THE LIGHT ON
ILLANCRONE

First published 1990 by
Poolbeg Press Ltd.
Knocksedan House,
Swords, Co Dublin, Ireland.

© Sean McMahon 1990

ISBN 1 85371 083 0

Cover design by Judith O'Dwyer
Printed by the Guernsey Press Ltd.,
Vale, Guernsey, Channel Islands.

THE LIGHT ON
ILLANCRONE

SEAN McMAHON

POOLBEG

For Joanne, who read it first

Contents

1
The Light on the Island

ey, boy!" said Ciaran, "there's a light on Illancrone."

"There couldn't be," I said. "It hasn't been inhabited for ten years. It is an uninhabited island."

"Well, have a look for yourself, my son."

Ciaran is a sort of mate but strictly for the summer months. For one thing he is English—from London—"Ealing, in fact, my boy!" Ciaran Aloysius Carter is his full name but we must be sympathetic. He is fond of talking as if he were a million years old and I some sort of kid. He comes over to Creagach every July and August. His father is a lecturer in Ealing College of Higher Education in law or something and his mother is a school nurse. She is very nice for an Englishwoman. You could see that she must

1

have been very attractive when she was young. His father, Paddy, was born in Letterkenny in spite of his name and he always tells us how he used to come to Creagach when he was a boy— as if we were interested in ancient history!

I got up from the table and walked to the window to see where he was pointing. Illancrone is a real island, entirely surrounded by very deep and often rough water. When people lived there they could be cut off for days because the strait was too dangerous for curraghs and there was no decent anchorage for half-deckers. Creagach where we stayed is only an island at full-tide and even then you can use the road-bridge at the south end.

As we looked out it was actually a bit hard to tell whether there was a light or not. There were really black clouds building up but the last rays of the sun shone like searchlight beams straight at the town. It's not really a town, just a winding street of houses. That was the sort of local expression that used to make Ciaran laugh at the start. He'd arrive in Creagach, fancying himself as a great scientist and detective, full of smart cracks and trying to speak like Jeremy Brett. He'd call me "my dear Watson" if I gave him half a chance but he is small, wears glasses and sounds more like Barney Rubble. My name is Gary O'Donnell, by the way, and I was fifteen in May.

Ciaran in spite of very careful rearing believes the Irish are a bit wild. At least he thinks that for the first week of July. After that he becomes more Irish than the Irish themselves. I said that once to him in Latin; he was impressed. He knows a lot of scientific things, I must admit. When he first saw the strip fields on Illancrone he nodded wisely and said, "Rundale, of course."

We decided to walk to the point of Creagach nearest to Illancrone to have a proper look even though there was a storm rising. It was better than playing switch which is probably the most boring game in the world. I don't know for sure because I don't play chess; maybe that's the most boring game in the world. One of the few times I succeeded in silencing Ciaran was when I said I was too old to learn it. He was quiet for nearly a minute.

We took our anoraks because the wind was blowing hard from the south-west and there would soon be a lot of rain. Mother and Father and my young sister Jill were on their way from Derry. My father is a doctor, you should know, and he often takes surgeries even during the holidays. My mother teaches infants. Jill had to go to a hospital clinic about her tonsils but they expected to be back by ten. There was never any need to lock the cottage door. Creagach people are honest and they miss very little about the movement of visitors. Our family has been renting the same cottage from Oweney Frank from well before the time that Mary, my older sister, was born.

The lights were nearly all lit in the caravans as we passed the site and also in the tourist cottages that had been built on the height above Tráigh Dhearg, my favourite beach. They were usually taken by Dublin people and Germans and they were hardly ever empty during the season. The storm was gathering in, as the local people say. Tory light which you could just see to the north-east was very bright because the sky was darkening from the west and the wind which is hardly ever less than four or five was up to seven and rising. The sky grew inkier and a few black tatters of cloud, like wool a black sheep might leave on barbed wire, were being fairly birled along.

We crossed by the swan lake which they say has rainbow trout though I never caught any, nor did my father. We climbed up the hill to get the best view of Illancrone, passing a little hollow that I christened the Hare's Nest because I used to see them there leaping and bundling about the grass. Sometimes I'm brilliant like that.

At the top the wind nearly knocked us flying. It distorted our faces, flattening the skin or puffing out our cheeks if we half-turned to hear ourselves speak. Ciaran looked like the Zarg from Planet X and from his reaction I suppose I must have looked dire as well. Illancrone looks on the map as if a bit of Creagach had broken off and floated clear. In fact it is very different: there are no fine sandy beaches and no proper slip, and its twin tops are much higher than anything on Creagach. There are, too, very high cliffs on the northern side and inlets like mini-fjords.

As the year goes on the sun seems to set further to the west. At the end of June it shines between the tops and blinds you at sunset. You can see very little of the houses and fields. It was now getting on for the end of August and the last rays came over the shoulder of the western hill and played like a theatre spotlight on the town. That was why we could not be sure whether we had seen a light or not. The wind was making our eyes stream and we could feel the first drops of rain.

"Can you see anything?" I shouted.

We stared with soaked faces and bleary eyes at the island.

"No! the place seems as dead as ever." The wind and rain were really fierce now and we signed to each other that we should get shelter before we were really wrecked. The blast dropped for a second as it sometimes does before a really massive gust. Ciaran shook my arm and pointed away from the town.

"Look at the old school."

That building was well away from the rest of the houses along a road that ran east to the end of the island. I looked. There was definitely a light in it whatever the power source. We blinked a few times to clear what Ciaran calls our "optics." There was no doubt. There was a light and therefore people on Illancrone. My father had told me once that for some years after the houses were abandoned the Illancrone people spent part of the summer "in" as they called it. It was handy for collecting dulse and carrageen and for checking lobster pots but since that time it was a desert island.

We ran down the hill and headed for home, Ciaran to his caravan, I to the cottage. The rest were in and there were hot pancakes for supper. No one was interested in the strange light on Illancrone so I stopped talking about it. The storm blew hard all night. At least it was still rattling the windows and making the rafters creak when I woke for a moment at first light.

2
The Girl on the Rock

By morning, though the gale was moderating, the sea by Tráigh Dhearg was mountainous. The sand and bent in the hollow were covered with a brown scum, a mixture of grit and spume. Illancrone looked much as it always did though there was white water all the way out the bay. There was no sign of Ciaran—great detectives don't get up very early—but there was smoke from some of the holiday cottages. I decided to risk a swim from Tor Mór where the water was only jabbly. I was just about to dive in when I heard a scream. There was a girl on Tor Mór and with the rising tide she was being drenched and what was more, knocked about. I'm no hero but at least I knew where the low water casán to the big rock lay. I kept the line feeling the smooth stones with my feet while the Tráigh Dhearg waves did their best to send me flying. The girl screamed again.

"Hilfe! Help me, please!"

German, I thought. She must be staying at the cottages.

"Sei nicht furchtbar!" I roared. "Ich komme."

I could see her plainly now. She had landed in the water and was trying to hold on to the rock. The waves were beating her against the jagged edges and I could see that her hands were bleeding. She was wearing a long T-shirt over her bathing-suit, a strange device I never could understand.

"Let go and swim to me!"

She stared at me with very blue eyes.

"Lasse es fahren!" I roared above the noise of the wind and waves. "Und schwimm hinein! Zu Mir!"

She just clung there being battered.

"Ich kann nicht..." she gasped out of breath, "...gut schwimmen."

Another illusion gone. A blonde Aryan beast who wasn't a crack athlete.

I was now about five yards from her and fairly certain that the water was clear and deep enough for a dive. Underneath the water was fizzy as Seven-Up but I got near enough to reach her and help her up on to a little shelf. She was shivering as much with cold as with fear and no wonder, stuck on Tor Mór with wet clothes.

"Wir müssen; wir müssen..." I realised my German was not equal to the task. "Kannst du Englisch?" I asked sheepishly.

"Natürlich!" Illusion restored: all Germans are blonde and blue-eyed and even if they can't swim they can speak English like natives.

"There is a ridge that is only four feet under water—meter und halb—but we have to swim for it."

She shook her head as if she wanted to dislodge it from her neck.

"The flaming tide is rising!"

"Flaming? You mean it is on fire?"

"We can't stay here. The waves will start breaking over us soon and we'll drown—at least, you will!"

She shook her head again as her teeth began to chatter.

"All right!" I said with a sudden burst of inspiration, "Take off your shirt."

She looked at me as if I were some sort of creepie-crawlie but she pulled it off all the same.

"Right! We're going to twist your shirt into a rope, verstehst Du?, and I'll lower you into the water. Then when I tell you, take a deep breath and keep your mouth closed until I tell you to open it. I'm going to pull you over to the casán."

"Casán?"

"Never mind. Just slide in when I tell you."

She slid into the sea giving her thigh another long gash and disappeared under. I jumped in a little bit from her and for a few seconds we seemed to hang like weights on a pulley. The shirt rope had fouled and was hooked on a spike of rock. Her eyes were tightly closed so that was all right. The old brain never worked so fast. I let my end go, swam to her and pulled the shirt free. Then I started to swim backwards using my legs only. She actually began to move though it was hard going. My lungs were sore because I had to keep underwater for the space between her rock and the casán. At last I reckoned it was time to risk it. Still holding on to the shirt I turned on my stomach and could see the edge I wanted. I got my head clear and held on to the rock made a lot more jagged by sharp mussels. Ciaran says the rocks are granitic conglomerates and he may even be right. Amazing how many different ideas you can hold in the old head at the same time. The sleeve of the girl's shirt was under my left hand and with a lot of muscular effort and badly gashed knees I was able to climb out and sit holding her tethered as her head cleared the foam. Like myself she was massively out of breath but she was not scared any more. She just nodded her head as she gulped air into her lungs. It is a relief to do that but it is nearly as sore as having them empty.

"Are you…" I found it hard to speak. "Are you OK?"

"Ja," she panted, "OK!"

She was able with my help to climb up beside me and with far fewer wounds than me. As she calmly wrung out her shirt and tied it round she looked at me gravely.

"You have saved my life."

It was nearly a question. I shrugged my shoulders.

"Only from pneumonia."

"Bitte? Please? I do not understand."

"The tide never covers the very top of Tor Mór. You'd have been safe but very wet. The only danger with such a white sea running was that a wave might have knocked you off."

"Christa, Liebchen!"

There was someone calling from Tráigh Dhearg.

"Mütti! Bin sicher! Komm' gleich!"

She took my hand.

"Come. Meine Eltern. My parents are on the beach."

We waved and started for the strand. Christa was pretty nippy on her feet. By the time I jumped the last yard on to the rough sand she was wrapped in the biggest towel you ever saw. The parents were blonde too, the man wearing lederhosen (pants only!) and the woman jeans and a shirt like the girl's.

"Hier ist... Verzeihung! Wie heisst du? What is your name?"

"Gary O'Donnell."

We shook hands. I said, "Pleased to meet you!" in German.

"Herr O'Donnell, Sie sprechen Deutsch."

"Nur ein wenig!"

It was true: I knew only a little but I was very pleased and a bit shocked to be addressed as "Sie." Was I growing up at last?

Christa and her parents, who were called Weiss, began rattling away in German. I could understand very little of it but from the way Christa kept pointing at Tor Mór I assumed she was describing the daring rescue ha! ha! By this time my father and Ciaran and his father had joined the group and there was all that bright, friendly chat that older people seem not only to be good at but actually to enjoy. I was beginning to introduce Ciaran to Christa when her mother who, it seemed was Rechtsanwältin—a solicitor—said that Christa needed dry clothes and hot soup. So with a lot more chat and promises to meet soon they moved off.

"Come to Number Seven at fourteen hours," called Christa.

It sounded so militaristic I almost saluted.

3

Someone on the Island

hat afternoon we sat on the spink above the east end of Tráigh Dhearg eating ice-cream with raisins that Christa's mother had made—a great delicacy, it seems, in Passau. Ciaran was being very grand comparing what he called the educational systems of their two countries. I was happy to sit with my back well supported by a comfortably weathered rock and half-listened with eyes closed to their chat. The sun was warm, we were full of German cooking and we didn't have to move for hours.

"Cripes!" whispered Ciaran, "look at Illancrone, boy!"

The day was clear enough to see the street of houses in fair detail.

"What?" I asked impatiently. "I can see

nothing." Then a bit grandly, "Ich kann nichts sehen."

Christa made a little face of mockery which suddenly turned my legs to water.

"Look! Just beyond the school."

As I said the school on Illancrone was well away from the "town." It was really the last house to the east apart from a derelict byre and very close to the high cliffs at that end of the island. I looked where he was pointing and maybe I saw something and maybe I didn't.

"Has your father got binoculars?"

"Bitte?"

I mimed with curled fingers.

"Ach, ja! Feldstecher! But why ask whether father has them. Why not Mutti?"

The last thing I needed was a lecture on feminism.

"Bloody well get them; we can argue about sexual stereotyping later!"

She smiled as she jumped up.

"Jawohl! mein Kapitän!" and again I felt weak at the knees. Was this love at last? She was back in two seconds and handed the glasses to Ciaran.

"Ah!" he said in his most annoying Baker Street voice, "Just as I expected. Was my original proposition not correct? There are people on that rocky outpost!"

I took the glasses from him and focused on the schoolhouse. There was certainly someone there—a man—and from the way he held his head he was certainly talking to someone else.

"Bitte," said Christa. "Let me look please." She put the Feldstecher to her eyes. "I see nothing."

I got behind her and, putting my hands on top of hers, I turned her face round till it pointed roughly at the school. Her hands were soft and I kept my own on hers for longer than was necessary. Suddenly she gasped and shook me off.

"Ach, du lieber…!"

"What is wrong, my child?" asked Sherlock Carter! "You've gone quite pale."

She lowered the binoculars. "It is nothing. I'm just suddenly cold."

"Ah! It's reaction to your dangerous morning! You are probably a little bit shocked."

"Vielleicht."

She handed me the glasses again. I scanned the whole island from west to east but couldn't get a sighting. There was a gas cylinder outside the school but there was no sign of a curragh or boat about the water's edge. Of course I was seeing only the front side of a square and a little bit of each side and there were plenty of deep coves where you could hide a craft.

"Who the hell are they?" asked Ciaran.

"The man I saw did not look like an islandman. Maybe he's a friend helping with lobsters."

"I think we should investigate. There is a mystery here that requires solution."

"Ecoutez bien! my egregious sleuth. It is a Kartoffel too hot to handle."

I sometimes talk like this to shut him up.

"It's either the IRA or drugs and little boy detectives should not meddle with big guys' games."

Christa did not even smile.

"Anyway," I continued "you can be bloody sure that the Creagach people will know all about it. Ask John Johnny Beag or Oweney and they will have the whole story."

Christa broke her Teutonic silence. "Drugs I understand but what is this IRA?"

Scarcely had she finished speaking when Ciaran launched on a history of Ireland from St Patrick to C J Haughey. And who better? The English always know more about Ireland than the mere inhabitants. I lay back and closed my eyes. I dozed a little. Through waves of sleep I could hear Christa politely saying "Yes, Ja." It was not until the great detective reached Baader-Meinhof in his lecture that Christa, who was on home ground at last, began actively to disagree with him. I could not let my patron be floored by a mere Fraülein, especially when she was in the right. Besides, Ciaran isn't all that much at ease with girls. I spoke.

"I gotta great idea: let's go to Aranmore."

Ciaran exhaled like a burst balloon.

"What's Aranmore?" asked Christa.

"Do you want the complete spiel or just the highlights?"

"Where is it?"

We pointed out the north cape of the big island where it lay like a great whale to the west of Illancrone.

"It's just a place to go. We can have a picnic and look at Pollnarone where the seals are."

"And the man from Atlantis will demonstrate yet again his amazing aquatic skills."

I looked at my watch. "If we are ready in fifteen minutes we can make the strand and get the bus at the Post Office."

"I must ask my parents," said Christa, "and how much money will I need?"

"My dear," said Ciaran grandly, "we will handle the financial arrangements."

"Nein. It is preferable that I pay for myself."

I shrugged my shoulders for the second time that day.

"Sort it out among yourselves and meet me at the graveyard in a quarter of an hour."

4
A Trip to Aranmore

e nearly missed the bus at Killaden Post Office. The tide had turned and left the sand quite hard and dry except for the deep channel at Gortladen. We raced across from Creagach to the edge. I must admit Christa could run. In fact I had the suspicion that she could have passed us if she had wanted to and she had certainly no difficulty keeping up with us. The water in the channel was about knee-deep but it was only a few yards across. I slipped off my sandals and started into the water but the others made no move. I turned to see what was keeping them. Christa had gone quite pale.

"Ich kann's nicht! I am sorry but I cannot."

Ciaran shrugged his shoulders. It was sure a day for it. She was wearing flip-flops. I took them and stuck them in the pockets of my shorts. "Now close your eyes, put your arms round our shoulders, move when I say, and don't open your eyes till I tell you."

It went fine though she did scream once: "Ach, Gott! Unter'm Fuss!"

Even Ciaran got impatient: "It's only a sand-eel."

Anyway we made it and we were soon swaying and jerking round the rugged roads of the Rosses. The bus as usual stopped about every five yards while pensioners out for their free rides climbed stiffly up and down the steps. I reckoned I would hate to be that old and said so, very quietly. Christa reproved me, saying that I should be old myself someday, which struck me as about the most blindingly original remark I ever heard. When we got to Dungloe the driver got out. This gave me a chance to run into Bonar's for three packets of crisps. Christa shook her head and said they were bad for teeth and practically everything else except maybe toe-nails. She ate the damn things all the same. At last the driver returned and drove us the five miles to the Port. We flew past the ruined coastguard station and the disused Protestant graveyard at fifteen miles an hour and turned into the harbour dock in time to see the Macha pull away from the quay.

"Donnerwetter!" I swore.

Christa looked mildly amused. We sat down on the harbour wall and watched the oil patches forming on the surface of the water. A heavy-duty catamaran dinghy with an outboard chugged across. I could sense that Ciaran was about to do his Sherlock bit. He was right, of course. You could easily get across to any of the islands on a job like that and you could beach it practically anywhere.

"You know, slaves—" he started when a voice behind us made him stop.

"How's the lads?"

It was Mickey Rodgers, an Aranmore fisherman that we knew because he used to fancy my big sister.

"Are ye goin' in? I've a few crates and boxes to load for Philly but we'll not be long behind the Macha."

We helped him load his half-decker, the Macha II. It used to be called Réalt na Mara but when the new ferry was commissioned he renamed it. He had that kind of humour. We settled Christa down amidships where she would get least rocking and not much spray. I could see she was surprised that we did not put on life-jackets. I explained it wasn't customary on these safe boats. Ciaran made a big deal of untying the rope from the jetty ring and pushing the boat out from the wall with his feet before jumping on to the deck.

Mickey let me take the tiller and I could not help noticing the impressed look on Christa's face. Ciaran was staring over the side looking down into the oily green water, no doubt collecting material for his future monograph on the fifty million types of algae to be found in the coastal waters of West Donegal. We passed between Inishcoo and Inishfree smoothly enough. Sometime I'll write my monograph on the fifty million islands called Inishfree. Still there are a lot of islands and there is a lot of heather, so why not as Barry Norman would say.

When we cleared Eighter we had about two miles of open sea to cross to get to Aranmore. The wind was light but the sea was still running a heavy swell. The Macha II began to pick up and dance on the waves. It is the loveliest feeling in the world but my companions did not seem to think so. Mickey came out from under the half-deck to guide her past the Stags—a parcel of nearly submerged, damnably sharp rocks. I stepped across to Christa and pulled her to her feet in spite of her "Nein! ich danke!" and made her sit with me right at the prow with our backs against the unused wheelhouse window. It always came as a shock to me how inexperienced inland, not to say Festland, people were about boats and the sea. Christa was from Passau and I am quite sure she could walk blindfold across a Tyrolean glacier without turning a blonde hair but here she was out of her element and certainly would agree with that swine Orlando in *As You Like It*.

"Yet I am inland born and know some nurture."

Ciaran says that anything I write is too full of literary allusions: he wouldn't know a literary allusion if it bit him on the foot.

Christa was a bit nervous at first especially when the odd drop of spray flew off the prow and hit us. She soon got used to the life of the boat on the water. She sat back and relaxed, laughing and whooping when we hit a bigger roller.

By now we were very near Aranmore. We could see the jetty with the Macha tying up and crowds of tourists waiting to leave. Higher up you could see the island roads with tractors and the odd battered VW grinding about. To the north was Illancrone and Ciaran's mysterious light and the men came into my head again.

"That's the island we were looking at earlier."

She nodded.

"You saw something, didn't you?"

She bobbed her head again.

"You knew the man with the blue cap?"

"He is my mother's cousin."

"And what's he doing here?"

"I don't know; we haven't seen him for several years. He is a scamp. Is that the word? Not a criminal but a little foolish."

"It's quite a coincidence his turning up here."

"Not a coincidence at all. He will perhaps have heard that Vati and Mutti are coming here."

She fell silent again but I could see that she was relieved to have talked about it.

The boat was gliding neatly to the new pier of Aranmore and with a lot more grace than Ciaran had ever managed she skipped with the rope on to the ground and tied up. Ciaran made fast the aft rope and I jumped off too.

"Take Christa to the Bialann and get her a Coke. I'll help Mickey unload."

"We will help," said Christa but Mickey cut in: "Never mind, darlin'. The tractor's not here yet and Gary and I can do the job ourselves."

I looked after them as they strolled up the

pier to the café. They made quite a contrast, the girl tall and slender and blonde with the longest slimmest legs I had ever seen, while Ciaran looked just silly with his green-visored golf-cap, his glasses and his very hairy legs. Mickey and I began laying off the plastic bales of milk cartons.

"Who's on Illancrone, Mickey?"

He looked at me sharply. I could see he was hesitating.

"Come on now. You know as well as I do that nobody moves about these islands without the locals knowing all about it."

"Ah now, Gary, I wouldn't say that."

"Are there Germans on the job?"

He nodded.

"Any locals?"

He shook his head. "...But Paddy Sharkey says there's a Dublin man interested in looking at Illancrone houses. But say nothing for the time being." He looked at me for a while. "What are you so interested for?"

"Anyway, run on now to your friends. Who's the girseach? Anything doing there?"

I smiled as mysteriously as I could. "She's German, staying at the cottages."

He smiled back. "Well, the best of luck to ye."

I ran up to the café where the other two were

deep in conversation. Or rather Ciaran was lecturing and Christa was listening with great attention. I suddenly felt excluded. It was quite a shock to find that I was jealous. I wondered again: was this love, at last?

"Trí uachtar reoite," I said to the girl behind the counter.

"Chocolate or raspberry?"

So much for the future of Irish as a living language, I thought.

5
The Indian from Glasgow

ein! I cannot eat another bite," cried Christa as I reached the table.

"Fear not my continental friend," responded Ciaran. "I am more than fit for every ice-cream you can throw my way."

"Aye or crisps or chocolate or husks!"

"What please are husks?"

Ciaran looked at me: "Well, literary genius, what are husks?"

"I'm not sure but in the Parable of the Prodigal Son it says he lived on the husks the swine did eat."

"So," said the great sleuth, "which am I? Prodigal Son or swine?"

Even Christa caught that one.

There was not a cloud in the sky when we left the Bialann and headed for Pollnarone.

Aranmore seems in places to rise sheer from the sea and unless you are travelling along its length you have to climb very steep roads. Christa kept stopping to look at flowers and discussing their stupid names with Ciaran. Every so often she would look at me and smile as if to say: "interesting as I find this botany lesson, it is you I'm really interested in." At least that is what I read into it. Ciaran seemed not to know she was a girl. How dumb can you get!

We crossed a few stiles, listened to a lecture on turf and the best way to make a stack and finally reached the shingly beach of Pollnarone. The water is very clear there and the "poll" itself is very deep. Christa went behind a rock and a nano-second later she was in her cossie, a word I left the Ealing brain to explain while I stood on a flag beside the hole and made ready to dive in.

I suppose I was showing off a little and I could sense Christa's admiration or, to tell the truth, I was hoping for her admiration. Anyway, once I was in and heading down to the bottom of the hole I did not care whether anybody was impressed or not. There is something about a header into a clear, clean pool that makes a lad feel great. The only trouble was that the water was so buoyant that I was stopped halfway

down and started rising again, feet first. I
turned and zipped up again to the surface and
climbed out to mild applause.

"You got down quite far that time, nicht
wahr?"

I nodded.

"Perhaps you will bring me something from
the bottom?"

"Bestimmt!"

I stood on the rock again and made one of
those up and down dives that nearly wreck your
back. It worked, though, and it kept me near the
the rocks that formed the walls of the hole. I got
down to about a yard from the bottom, though
I supposed I should say metre for Christa's
sake. I grabbed a fat frond of kelp and used it to
pull me down to the shelly floor. It was as clear
as if I were wearing a mask. Then I saw just
what I was looking for: a sea-urchin case, nearly
perfect and about the size of a pineapple. I
grabbed it and it came away easily. I put my feet
together, let my knees flex and headed for the
top.

I broke the surface, put the shell down
carefully and shook the water out of my ears
and eyes. As I gasped to try to recover normal
breath I realised that there was a lot of shouting
going on and screaming too. The man Christa

had recognised on the island was trying to carry her down to a catamaran dinghy which had somehow come into the cove.

"Lass das sein, Günter! Geh weg! Verschwinde!" she shouted.

Ciaran, who had a bloody nose, was clinging like a monkey to a heavy man with an aran sweater and jeans and wearing a red cap (of Ciaran's sort) with Detroit Indians woven on the front. It's amazing what the mind can take in in a second. Long before I had finished thinking I was rushing at Günter with my head down and roaring like a bull. "Let her alone, you bastard!" My head hit his stomach as I burst between them. The momentum (mass by velocity, measured in newton-seconds) carried us both for several metres until he fell with me on top of him. I was nearly sick with the pain in my head and my nose felt like a squashed tomato. Still from the dirty white colour of his face I knew he felt worse than I did. I rolled away and not a moment too soon for Christa had picked up a rock as big as a plain loaf and seemed about to brain him.

"Ah wudnae advise that, hen!" cried the Detroit Indian in a Glasgow accent you could have chipped off with a chisel. The only response was a flash of lightning from her eyes.

She could not see that the Glasgow Indian had picked Ciaran up by the back of the neck and did not seem about to wish him a Happy Hogmanay. Günter was holding his hands in front of him as if Christa's rock were a football and he was trying to save a penalty. I stood between them looking from one frozen figure to the other. I reached for a stone like Christa's but I was not very sure what to do with it. A long minute passed.

"Ahm gonnae smash this wee mannie's heid!"

He did a neat juggling trick and while admittedly a bit red in the face was still able to hold poor Ciaran's head about a foot above the ground. He seemed ready to use him like an old fashioned navvy's tamper.

I didn't have a clue what to do. Two heads, neither of them mine, looked about to take a knock. Then the spell was broken by a motor horn. Everyone except Christa turned to look. It was the postie and he was stopped up on the road. Never did a green and yellow van look so welcome.

"Let's go, McBirnie," rasped Günter and ran towards the dinghy. McBirnie laid Ciaran down quite gently on the shingle. I probably only imagined his sigh of regret. Christa looked at

me uncertainly. I nodded vaguely and she
dropped the stone. McBirnie rasped the cord of
the outboard and they sped out of the cove.
Christa sat down on a rock and covered her face
with her hands. Ciaran was up now, shaking
his head and feeling his physog for damage. I
just felt cold in spite of the heat of the sun. The
great detective spoke first:

"Well! What was that about?"

Christa's face was still hidden. Ciaran stared
at her. I just stood there trying to stop
shivering. "I'm going to get dressed."

After a long while Christa spoke. Her
English had deteriorated. "I am afraid that my
mother's cousin is bad. He is in evil business
and he does not want my mother to know about
it."

"Drugs, I suppose," said Ciaran calmly.

"I don't know."

"Guns?" I asked. "Semtex?"

Christa began to cry. It was Ciaran who
produced an amazingly clean handkerchief and
with soothing cries was dabbing her eyes. I felt
like a right eejit.

"It seems clear to me that these are hard men
and they are up to something," said Ciaran.
"Yet though they could have flattened us they
didn't." (He was well away now. I was almost

sorry that he hadn't a pipe or at least what his hero called a "lens.") "Their purpose, it would seem, was more or less to kidnap Christa." He sat back, quite pleased with himself. We both looked at her. This time she did not lower her gaze.

"I do not think he would hurt you—nor me. Perhaps he does not wish my parents to know that he is here. I think that he and his comrades are smuggling something."

"And there's an Irish connection?" asked Ciaran.

"I do not think that he is a terrorist. It is something else and I think it is going to happen quite soon."

"What, then," asked Ciaran, "should we do?"

"Nothing, Nichts, Rien, Faic!" I almost shouted, speaking for the first time.

"We should tell the police," said the law-abiding Brit.

"Tell them what? That there's some stir on Illancrone? That Christa's cousin, whom she hasn't seen for three years, wanted her to go with him. We have nothing to tell the guards. Can you imagine the look the desk-sergeant in Dungloe would give you?"

"We should keep an eye on Illancrone," insisted Ciaran. "That's where the key to this mystery lies."

"We should walk away, get on with our holiday and not play silly beggars, as your mother has said to us in the past."

Christa nodded. "You have right. Sorry, you are right."

"And," I said, "to make sure, we'll go to Loughanure tomorrow to fish and hope that those jokers keep well away."

6
The One That Didn't Get Away

oughanure is about nine miles from Creagach over very narrow bog roads. At breakfast I mentioned a possible trip to the lake. I was afraid that my father would think it too good an idea and want to come.

"You know, Gary," he said, "that's a very good idea. I wouldn't mind a nice spot of fishing myself."

I looked at Mother. She smiled and winked behind his back. "Sure we have to go to Pettigo to pick up Mary, but what you can do is to give the lads a lift. I suppose Ciaran's going?"

"Yes and that German girl beyond in the cottages."

"The one you were rescuing from Tor Mór?"

"Mother!"

"Well" said Father with a sigh, "You can take

the old fly-rod and make yourself a cast for trawling. And I suppose that means that I'll have to do your dishes again."

"Well, mate, I did yours twice last week!" I said and then ducked. Jill said as usual, "I want to go too." and I said as usual, "You're too young and too big a nuisance," and Mother said as usual, "Never mind, dear. You can come with us and meet Mary at Lough Derg. And we'll have our lunch in Donegal Town—"

"Except Mary of course—"

"—except Mary naturally, and then when we come back you can go and play with the young Sweeneys."

Jill smiled as usual; she loves hotel meals and she's not a bad wee thing really.

Ciaran was lying in front of their caravan looking at a flower through—yes, you've guessed it!—a lens! His mother buys him everything.

"What did you make of that business yesterday?" he asked.

We hadn't talked much on the way home. We were kind of shook. Christa was relieved to see that the Macha was waiting. She had had enough excitement that day and she had gone home to the cottage as soon as we had got back to Creagach, on the back of a sand-lorry, as it happened. Ciaran has about as much tact as an elephant and he insisted on walking with us right to the edge of the casán that led to the cottages' enclosure.

"Good night! and thank you both," she said very sweetly. Not for the first time I wished Ciaran would get lost.

"I don't know what to make of it," said I. "Those were a tough pair of guys."

"What do you think they're up to?"

"Smuggling of some sort, I expect, but they are bloody silly if they think they're not noticed on Illancrone."

We walked up the black road to the cottages. The sea was very blue and Errigal and Cnoc Fola looked faded. The Tráigh Dhearg rocks glowed red. It struck me that summer would soon be over.

"Me da says he'll take us over to Loughanure about twelve and pick us up again about four."

"Magic!" said Ciaran looking at a lump of rock through his lens.

"We'll have his old fly-rod and a line with a cast for trawling."

"Super!" he said, picking at the stone.

"Will your parents let you come?"

"No problem!"

I had the feeling I was talking to myself. We

had reached the door of Number Seven which, oddly enough, was shut. I knocked and Frau Weiss opened the door. She smiled.

"Kommt herein!... Christa!... Deine Freunde."

She led us into the living-room, and there was—Günter! He looked at us with great interest. Ciaran started so speak but I dunted him in the ribs and by the time he had recovered Christa was there and we were on our way out.

"Mutti is very glad to see him." she said. "He told her he had seen us on the island yesterday. When she went to make coffee he said he was sorry for being so rough."

"Rough?"

"Ja, rough. He said he was a little bit drunk and was quite shocked to see me."

"Do you believe him?"

She shrugged.

"Anyway, let's go fishing. Mutti has made sandwiches and cookies."

"And I'm bringing two big bottles of pop."

We let Christa travel in front with my father so that he could bore her with a guided tour. She was a good actress that one, because she appeared genuinely interested and it pleased the old man greatly. At the lake the weather wasn't bad for fishing. It had got a bit cloudy and there was a good "top." We decided, or rather, I decided to row up against the breeze to the top of the lake and drift down again. Christa sat in the stern looking slightly scared and Ciaran kept squeaking about something or other at the sharp end.

We got right up to the south end of the lake without so much as a rise. I had played out a bit of the line from the old trout rod and let it drift behind us. Christa was a little bit nervous about having the rod beside her but it never moved. We turned and let the boat cruise down in the slight breeze. I put Christa and Ciaran to bailing with flattened dried-milk tins while I tried a few casts. I'm no Isaak Walton but I have been lucky in the past. Christa watched with great serious interest which I read as a form of admiration. Some of the casts were quite well done, classical throws. Then I had one! The line buzzed out and Christa gave a little cry. I did all the right things: I kept my elbow into my side, held the tip high and mixed giving slack and reeling in until finally a neat trout was scrabbling in the water and practically climbing into the boat. Ciaran is pretty cool about net work and in a second a half-pound brown was skittering about the bilge. Christa kept screaming as Ciaran tried to catch it. I noticed she looked away when I was taking out the fly. At least she sat still and didn't risk overturning the boat. I handed the rod to Ciaran, grabbed the boyo and had his neck broken before anybody knew.

Then the other reel began playing out. We had wedged it between the stern boards leaving the handle free to turn. The cast was one that usually worked on Loughanure but we didn't really expect to pick up anything without a rod. Ciaran moved very neatly for him and sat beside Christa at the back. Then he manoeuvred her round to sit amidships. He held the reel very firmly in place and began winding in. I could tell from the tension in the line that we either had a whale or a piece of weed, and when it suddenly went slack and he wound up the cast we could see that weed was what it was. At least the flies were still on the cast. We laughed a lot.

There was a patch of shingle near the north end and we beached there for lunch. Christa was learning the drill: she hopped over the edge into the water, not seeming to mind the stones or the grit. Ciaran was able to land with dry feet. As we ate the food the sun came out. It was an obvious time to talk about our adventures and I knew I could rely on Ciaran to be tactless enough to start.

"It was a bit of a shock, seeing old Günter there." he said.

"Old?" said Christa frowning, "He is not yet thirty." Nobody bothered to explain and she continued. "He was just there at the door this morning. My mother was so pleased to see him. He says he is working with an—what is the word for bringing in goods?"

"Importing."

"Ja, an importing business in Dublin."

"Bigod, he's right there lads!"

Ciaran had become very Irish indeed but his English vowels had not changed. The effect was as he might have said in one of his grander moments, "decidedly odd!"

"Importing what?" I asked.

"He did not say."

"Well, now that he has come out he will leave you alone."

"All the same," said the great detective, "There is definitely something going on!"

"So there is and it's none of our flaming business!"

He dug into his bag for more food and brought out a small cardboard packet.

"What the hell is this?"

It was blue with a loose paper label and the

word MULTILIT printed on it. He tried to get us interested but there was nothing in it.

"Maybe you picked it up somewhere. What difference does it make? Throw it away!"

Christa caught it and stuffed it back in his bag. "Take your litter home!"

We piled back into the boat. Christa and Ciaran both wanted to row so I let them. After about five minutes of zig-zagging and once turning right round that caused a lot of merriment they finally got it straight and we moved fairly speedily up the lough again. I sat at the back like a caliph or a Roman emperor being transported by slaves. I could not help looking at Christa's fair hair which glinted in the sun as it periodically came out from behind the clouds. It contrasted sharply with Ciaran's mouse. Am I at last in love, I wondered again. It was a strange feeling, not entirely pleasant. I felt nervous and elated at the same time. I felt jealous and flattered all at once and when her serious face broke into a smile my heart turned over.

Suddenly the reel of the rod which I had propped beside me over the sternboard rattled. I lifted it and felt a satisfactory tension. "Keep rowing, slaves!" I called as I began to wind in. The tension in the line increased and I tried to remember what my father had told me about when to give a sporting fish line. I switched the ratchet, gave about a metre or two and began reeling in again. There was still a marked bend in the rod but the tension was easing. There was a flash of silver as it broke the surface and I thought for a minute that I had lost it. Then I reeled again hard and it came in.

Now was the tough part. The galley slaves were still rowing mightily so I had to use the landing net myself. It was fortunately a spring loader and with great good luck I managed to lift the trout into the boat. She was a beauty; at least a pound, a fine white trout so lively that it was in danger of jumping out of the boat again. Christa was impressed though she turned her head away when I put my thumb in its mouth and bent the head back.

We were doing well. The white trout made the brown one we had caught before lunch seem very puny indeed. You never know with fish. Some days there is no hope—most days in fact. I had a good feeling about this day, somehow. We turned at the top and began to drift down again. Well, they practically jumped into the flaming boat. By the time we were halfway down we had ten, some of them only just fit to keep but very tasty. We laughed and sang.

Christa did not mind the smell nor the way the scales clung to her legs.

It went quiet again and we drifted. After a while we could see the car at the landing-stage. I graciously allowed the crew to bring us in. I had put our catch in a supermarket bag and handed it to Christa putting my finger on my lips. We jumped out, took the rowlocks and walked up to the car.

"No luck?"

I shook my head mournfully. Then Christa produced the bag from behind her back and every body laughed. My father was very impressed, especially with the big one which I had begun to call Moby Dick.

"I've just had a brilliant idea," he said. "It's my turn to make the evening meal. We'll have a barbecue this evening."

"At our caravan," said Ciaran, "and we'll have all the families."

"Is Mary here?" I asked, not really very interested.

"No, we put her on the Derry bus. She has one or two things to do."

Mary has always one or two things to do. I know she wanted to see her boy friend, indeed I suppose I should say her fiancé. It would have been much handier if she had decided to marry

Mickey Rodgers. Still I was beginning to understand this love business a bit better.

Later that evening we cooked the trout on the Carters' barbecue and ate them with rye bread that Christa's parents had brought. We sat round the fire and sang. Even Jill was allowed to stay up late. Christa and I sang "Muss i denn" as a duet and then it was time to go home. My parents helped the Fishlocks clear away and no one would let the Weisses do anything. They were guests. They rose to go.

"Komm mal! Christa."

"Zwanzig Minuten noch, Mutti, bitte!"

"Viertel Stunde, nichts mehr!"

"Jawohl."

Ciaran went inside and there was no one left but the two of us.

"I suppose we should go."

"Let us walk by the sea."

There was a smoky light in the sky and one or two stars. As we walked by the water's edge the bubbles were phosphorescent. We were too quickly at the cottages but I had time to show her the place I called the Hare's Den. At her door we stopped and looked at each other. She put her arms round my neck and kissed me. I had never really kissed before. I used to wonder where the noses went. But that kiss was wunderbar! She ran into the cottage. I don't remember any details of the walk back home.

7
The White Mercedes

I awoke next morning about eight o'clock. The *Complete Short Stories of Sherlock Holmes* was beside the bed. My father liked them nearly as much as Ciaran and it was one of the books as well as the *Complete Shakespeare* that stayed in the cottage. I read the one called "A Scandal in Bohemia." It was all right, I suppose. It mentioned a lady called Irene Adler. "To Holmes she is always the woman." Funny how I always skipped bits like that before. It was the one case where Holmes was foiled. "The best plans of Mr Sherlock Holmes were beaten by a woman's wit." I heard my father's car drive off and Jill open her door to play with her dolls on the cement bit in front that would have been called the terrace in a posher house. I read a bit more of Sherlock

Holmes and then went to the bathroom when Mother called.

When I got to the kitchen the toast was ready. It's really amazing the appetite you get by the sea. I took two bowls of cornflakes, three rounds of toast and about a gallon of tea.

"Are you going to Tráigh Dhearg this morning?" asked Jill. "If you are, I'm coming too."

"No! he's not." said Mother, "He has to go to Dungloe to pay the ESB bill."

"Can I come too?" yammered Jill. "I want to go to the Cope to get another book."

She is quite bright, my young sister—reads about a book a day. I suppose it is because she is five and a half years younger than me and used to playing by herself. Mind you, she's not strange, though she tends to take Glinka, her toy bear ("He's not a teddy!") with her everywhere. She has lots of mates at home but unless there is some kid among the visitors about her own age she's on her own. Sometimes she is allowed to play with a local family called Sweeney, as long as she "isn't a nuisance!"

"No, he'll take the bike. You'd never make the early bus now. I'll give you the money for two books. Is it still the Fearless Five?"

"Yes, Mammy, but not *The Fearless Five Beat*

the Smugglers. I have that. There's still *The Fearless Five on Curlew Island* I haven't got."

Mother gave me a list of messages as long as your arm: *The Derry Journal*, *The Irish Times*, *Woman's Life*, sausages, butter, cake and on and on. It's a good thing the bike had a big bag.

There is something really great about cycling on a good morning especially if you haven't being doing it for a while. The main road—the only road, for Pete's sake—is very narrow and twists and turns like a snake. Cars, and there aren't all that many of them, have to go very slow and try to find a passing-place to get by each other. If you are on a bike and you find a car coming it is a bloody good idea to get off the road and stand on the ditch.

I flew along. The reeds by the Graveyard Lake are over seven feet high and they rustle even when there is no breeze. I used to hate passing there alone in the dark. So did the locals! This morning they waved like the sea and I was cycling like Stephen Roche. There was plenty of traffic on the Dungloe road but they were decent about the space they left for poor cyclists. The sun was warm on my face and I felt great. Dungloe was just waking up so I got the shopping done fairly quickly. I had some crack with Mickey Rodgers in the Cope. He was

buying barbed wire and staples and it took ages
to find the man, pick the right staples and load
the lot into his old VW van.

We talked about the usual things: the
weather—good; the fishing—nearly over; the
marquee—too old for me; and Christa (the wee
German thing). He did not mention Illancrone
at first and though I was bursting to I held off.
I thought it best.

"Much stir among the visitors?"

"The usual: daily golfers and the McGuigan's
speedboat."

"As far as I know. Any news from you?"

"Not, yet."

I left him at that and was about to head back
to Creagach when a minibus came into the main
street and parked by the bank. Out jumped
Ruairi Ó Bláine, or Roy Blayney, as he is for
most of the year. He is in my class at school and
good, as you might gather, at Irish.

"Caidé mar? mar dúirt an Indiach Dearg."

"Go measartha."

There was a girl with him, a brunette with
slightly buck teeth.

"Seo Máire as Baile Átha Cliath."

"Conas tá tú?" she said, lisping with her little
rabbity teeth. I love the crazy way Southerners
pronounce Irish.

"An raibh tú ag an gCéilí Mór i nGaoth Dobhair, oíche aréir?"

"Ní rev."

I fell apart laughing.

We went to the snack bar and had cokes—and talked mostly English. Then they had to go and so had I. Mind you I liked Máire as BAC. She was good crack in spite of her lisp and buck teeth and funny Irish—but she wasn't a patch on Christa.

I pushed my bike up the Fair Hill which was steep but not so windy as the main road, and was soon birling along. A car behind me began to toot so I pulled in right to the edge of the road which luckily had a high dry ditch on my side. It kept tooting and when I turned my head to look I began to wobble. The car accelerated and practically touched me. It was a white Mercedes with a Dublin registration but I couldn't make out the swine of a driver.

I cycled on, a bit shaken but not in jitters. It was getting very hot and the sun over my right shoulder was very glary. I was trying to decide whether to try to ride up the Lefin Brae or walk the first tough bit when suddenly out of a sidetrack the white Merc came straight at me. Everything seemed to happen very slowly like an instant replay in a TV broadcast of football.

I knew I had to brake or pedal like hell. If I braked I would certainly skid and fall; if I pedalled on he would surely hit me. As it was, I froze. The bike moved by itself and I just got across. The white car actually brushed my reflector. I shuddered to a stop. I was shaking. This time there was no mistake. He was trying to hit me, maybe even kill me. I pushed the bike slowly up the hill, trying to think. There was something bloody dangerous going on and I did not want to be part of it!

After a while I calmed down a bit. My stomach stopped doing jumps and my breath became normal again. I got on again and sailed down the hairpin-bends. I froze a little every time I heard a car but they all passed by without attempting to harm me. I was climbing up to the Hall, a very steep bit of road with a twenty foot drop on the left. Creagach was in view and I could see the end of Illancrone when I heard the race of the car and felt the push that tipped me over. I was riding on air and then I was falling. I felt a bang on my nose and then I felt no more, as they always say.

The next thing I remember was Mickey bending over me. My head was sore and my nose was bloody; it was taking quite a bit of punishment. Everything else seemed to be working. The bike was about two yards away and sitting upright in the soft wet sand! It looked in better nick than I did. Mickey helped me up. My head was throbbing and I felt a little bit sick.

"What happened?" asked Mickey as if he knew already.

"A guy in a white Mercedes kept edging me off the road. He finally succeeded."

Mickey nodded. "Are ye all right? Can ye walk?"

I put out each leg slowly and each arm. "I seem to be OK."

"Good man! Let's see to the bike."

He lifted up the front fork and twirled the wheel. It went as well as ever. I caught the saddle and spun the pedals. There was a spray of sand but otherwise things were fine. I looked in the bag and everything appeared all right. It was lucky that the Cope was out of large eggs. We carried the bike to the hard sand and then wheeled it up a kind of rough path to the road. Mickey opened the back door of his van and we pushed in the bike. In a few minutes we were crossing the bridge into Creagach.

"Don't mention this to my parents, Mickey!" I warned.

"No nor anyone else. Ye might drop a wee

hint to the German lassie to keep out of things."

"I already have!"

Mickey dropped me at the caravans and headed for Burtonport. "I'll be lookin' out for ye!"

I gave him the thumbs-up sign and pushed the the bike slowly and carefully up the casán. Mother was waiting.

"Was that Mickey Rodger's van I saw you get out of? What's his crack?"

"Nothing much," I said unloading the messages. She looked at me with the usual maternal concern.

"What happened your nose?"

"I fell off the bike at Lough Dubh."

"Are you all right? Is the bike all right? What about the eggs? You'll kill yourself some day!"

"There were no eggs."

"No eggs in the Cope?"

"You asked for large. The ones they had looked like pigeon's."

"Well," she said, "go and wash your face. I don't know. I just don't know!"

8
Drugs!

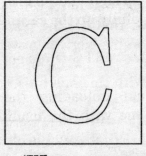

Ciaran was lying on Tor Mór looking at carrageen moss.

"Where were you all day?"

"I was in Dungloe for messages. Any word of Christa?"

"They're all away on a tour—you know, Glencolmcille, Killybegs, probably even Glenveagh too."

"We must go there someday."

"Yikes! like tourists?"

I nodded.

"What happened your hooter?"

"I fell off the bike."

"Drunk again!" He heard that expression from his father.

"Seriously though, I was pushed."

"By what?"

"By a white Mercedes with a Dublin registration."

"You didn't get the number?"

"No, except that it was registered last year in the capital."

He fished out of the pocket of his shorts which as usual were stuffed with rubbish the blue packet that he had found in his bag when we were at Loughanure.

"I think it is connected with this business."

"Let's have a look."

It was a blue package with the word MULTILIT on a white label that was hardly stuck on at all. The tab of the opening had what looked like a "use-by" date and the bottom was stamped "Brona GMBH, Dresden, DDR." I whistled.

"What is it?"

"It's from East Germany and it looks like some kind of medical drug, or (and here I had a brainwave) more likely veterinary!"

"What's GMBH?"

"Same as PLC. Do you want me to translate?"

"Don't bother!"

"Let's go and ask Anthony Doherty. He's a vet."

"And what'll we say?"

"We'll think of something."

Doherty lived on the mainland just across from the caravan-site though he had his surgery in Dungloe. He had a boat with a really powerful motor and he was decent about taking us out the bay in it. We headed off across the tide, though it was only up to our ankles and only really got deep at the tidal stream at the far shore. We walked up the path to the road and headed for the vet's house. We had to pass the fish-processing factory but we managed it without discomfort. Actually I quite like the smell but Ciaran says it makes him sick. Anthony's car was there and when we knocked Mrs Doherty brought us in and gave us lemonade. They have a couple of babies but they weren't produced.

"How's the lads?" said Anthony looking in.

"The best—and yourself, Anthony?"

"Couldn't be better!"

Ciaran cannot get used to the idea of calling adults by their first names.

"What can I do you for?"

We showed him the packet.

"Where did you come on this?"

"We found it round about Leabgarrow. Is it in your line?"

"It is and it isn't!"

We looked at him.

"It's in my line all right but we can't get it. It's a fertility drug for sheep and cattle. So I'd like to know where you got it."

All this time I let Ciaran do the talking, quite happy to sip the lemonade and let the gas tickle my damaged hooter.

"I must have picked it up when I was gathering other bits and pieces I'd dropped. It was probably when we were at Pollnarone. There's Germans above in the cottages."

Anthony shook his head doubtfully. "I don't think so."

Ciaran was looking at me knowingly. He may be a great detective but he's a lousy secret agent. I rose.

"We'll go now, Anthony," I said, "Thank Mrs Doherty for the treat."

"Thank her yourself; she's in the kitchen. What are you doing this evening?"

"Nothing." We waited expectantly.

"Like to come for a quick run? Not too far—round the back of Illancrone and home again. I have to be at a meeting in Dungloe at nine."

"Great, Anthony!" (Ciaran actually said "Super.") "Oh, by the way, we have a friend from one of the cottages, a German girl, she'd love to come."

"Bring her along. I'll take the Granuaile over

to the pier on Creagach about half-six. You can tell your mammy I'll have jackets for all of ye. Your friend will know to wrap up well. It will be cold enough round Illancrone."

We walked back across the sand drying now in the low tide. We reckoned we had time for a swim before tea and afterwards we lay on the cliff above the cottages waiting for the Weisses to come back. We were lying there half-asleep enjoying the afternoon sun. At least I was; Ciaran was thinking. I can always tell. He sat up and snapped his fingers.

"That's it!" he shouted.

"That's what?" I groaned.

"That's what they're doing: they're smuggling drugs."

"Waaoo!" I shouted, pretending to be really impressed.

"No, but don't you see? They'll bring this illegal Multilit in, take off the labels—you saw how loose the label was on the box we found—put on new ones maybe and sell them at a huge profits to chemists or vets."

"But the chemist or vet would need to be dodgy."

"Not necessarily; all it needs is one dodgy distributor—"

"And some vets who don't mind the law being

bent a little."

"Yes, yes," said Ciaran, "You're getting it!"

"I still don't see it. There must be controls and safeguards. No vet is going to use a drug he hasn't seen passed with all the tests done."

"True," said Ciaran in his best Baker Street style, "but suppose his supplier can show him that Multilit has passed all the East German tests and does work even though it's banned. Maybe it's only half the cost of the nearest EC equivalent. Some guys might think it their duty to buy the cheapest."

I felt a lecture about the EC and trade and all that sort of thing coming on so I ducked. "I still think we should keep out of it. They were a pair of tough boys; and what about the white Mercedes?"

"You didn't even see who was driving."

"Well, it's hardly a coincidence, my dear Holmes. I admit I have some nasty habits but I hardly deserve being shoved off the road, the state highway (Ciaran sniggered) by posh cars."

He grew silent. He was thinking again! Soon there would be a really wise remark.

"It must have been one of the gang!"

"Magnifique!" I cried. I'm not really interested in French but Ciaran doesn't know any German. It was risky, though: it was bad enough living with Sherlock Holmes. I did not need Hercule Poirot as well.

"I reckon they're going to bring in the stuff soon. They'll land it at the shingle beach and use the catamaran to bring it into Kinladen."

"Every man, woman, and eejit in this town will know all about it then! I'll bet they know something already. Men like Mickey Rodgers know everything that is going on. So who do they think they're fooling? The only hope they have is to have some local in the gang."

"Maybe they have," argued Ciaran, "How would they know about Illancrone without local advice?"

"I heard my father say that in the early seventies, about the time I was born, I suppose, all kinds of people were about Illancrone. Guys from Belfast and South Armagh and even Cricklewood, wherever that is."

"Why, it's not too far from—" said Ciaran anxiously.

"I was only kidding, man!" Sometimes Ciaran is too easy to tease!

"Garree! Garree!"

It was Jill's voice. She came cycling up, out of breath.

"Mammy says you're to take me and Christa to the Cowrie Beach."

I blinked.

"Yes!" she said smiling, "and you and her and Ciaran are to come for tea at six."

"Well for one thing, Smartie, Christa's not here yet, and for a second thing, Jillo, we have to be at the pier at six-thirty to meet Anthony Doherty."

"Is he taking you for a run? Oh, please, can I come? Please, please. I'll be good. I'll not talk too much. I'll say 'please' and 'thank-you.' I'll do the dishes when it's your turn next."

She paused, out of breath again. I looked at Ciaran. He nodded.

"Well it's really up to Anthony," I said, "and you'll need a life-jacket."

"I can easily borrow one from Mrs Sweeney."

"OK!" I said (I mean, she's not a bad kid.) "We'll just wait until Christa comes back and then—"

"But she's back already; she's up at the house drinking coffee."

We followed her on foot.

"Why do you want to go to the Cowrie Beach?" I asked when I got up to the house. I had left Ciaran at the caravans. I gathered he had some more detecting to do.

"Why, to gather cowries, of course."

"And what then? Stick them up our noses?"

Christa looked puzzled while Jill blushed and said I was rotten. She once had put one up her nose and we had to take her to Dungloe Hospital to get it taken out.

"I was only a little, tooty thing then. I have more sense now. Haven't I Christa?"

"Yes, naturally. We all do childish things when we are young. And, of course, Gary, if you do not want to come Jill and I will be all right on our own. You can show me the way by yourself, can't you, Jill?"

"Yes, certainly!" said Jill very grandly.

Mother broke in. "Right, Jill, off you go. Be careful at Scailp na Luinge. Stay on the path. The sand's very wet and soft even at this tide. And don't fall into any bog-holes."

She turned to me. "You can make yourself useful by washing potatoes, getting in turf, setting the table and tidying your room."

I opened my mouth to speak and, unable to think of anything to say, shut it again. The other two ran off laughing. I turned to look at Mother again. She meant it.

After about ten hours of heavy housework she let me go. I headed out along the road to Tráigh Mhuir na Mhaighdeog, as it was correctly named. There used to be a retired schoolteacher who lived in Creagach and he

told me the names of all the parts of the island.
I think he despised the regular tourists who
called places by their own not very interesting
names—Rat Island, Steep Bay. We called it the
Cowrie Beach because the right name is just a
little hard to say. The path I was on had been his
way down to the tarred road but after he died no
one used it and the grass was up to my waist in
places, awful on a wet day! The sun was lower
in the sky but still strong. I used to like that
when I was young. You walked with your eyes
filled with gold dust and everything was magic.
The west of Creagach has no sand except for a
tiny inlet that we called the other Tráigh
Dhearg because it had the same coarse sand.
The water is quite deep and you could easily get
a fair-sized boat in there at top tide. It is no good
for swimming, though, because it is black with
kelp and wrack and full of jelly-fish. The tide
was turning again but I could see marks of gum-
boots or waders and tracks of a keel. If Ciaran
had been there he could have drawn great
conclusions. To a simple man like myself it was
still clear that there had been a boat and men
there. The locals rarely used it since the two
tracks to it were very rocky and not suitable for
cars. A tractor could manage it, though. There
were no houses anywhere near and I

supposed... My thoughts trailed off.

I trudged on across the field where I once saw a parliament of rabbits down to the three strands of Scailp na Luinge which at high tide were covered except for the two rocky fingers that separated them. Creagach could be a very interesting place if a man knew something. By the time I had got up to the bog I could hear the girls coming. Jill was gabbling like mad and Christa was answering her very politely. She really was a very nice girl.

Jill cried, "Look, Gary, we've got hundreds."

She showed me her little clear plastic bag with the tiny pink shells. Christa had never seen cowries or venus shells before and she was examining the ridges and the cleft that looks like a mouth.

"They are like good china, no? Porcelain?"

I let the two of them rattle on and walked back along the path behind them.

"Tea will be ready when we get to the house. Salmon mayonnaise and Mother's brown bread."

"Great! shouted Jill, who had quite an appetite for a small girl. "Come on, Christa! Let's run!"

***

I told Ciaran and Christa about the tracks in the inlet as we walked down to the pier. Jill had run ahead to borrow a life-jacket. We wore pullovers and carried anoraks and made her go to collect her heavy gear. Ciaran explained his theory about the veterinary drugs. Christa looked serious—even more serious that usual. Her blue eyes were worried.

"It's just the sort of thing that Günter might be mixed up in. He is always looking for quick money and sometimes he does not care too much how he gets it."

"He has very rough friends." said I and told her about the white Mercedes.

"This is quite serious. Are you badly hurt?"

She seemed relieved to hear that I was still in one piece.

"In one piece! What a funny expression! Sehr komisch!"

"I expect they only wanted to frighten me." said I cheerfully.

"And succeeded, I'd say!" said Ciaran. "They practically broke your silly neck but sure it's hard to kill a bad thing!"

Christa looked cross.

"Gary is not a bad thing!" she said and caught his nose between her strong fingers.

"It's only an expression! Tell her, O'Donnell!"

"Say nothing yet to Anthony Doherty," I warned.

9
Round the Rugged Rock

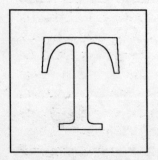he Granuaile was a
beauty, painted white
with an inboard motor
and capable of nine knots. Anthony was very
proud of her. He was easy to persuade to give a
body a run, at least now while his children were
very young. She raced across from Gortladen
liked a souped-up swan. The tide was half full.
He brought her into the tiny strand and we
helped the girls on board. Jill needed very little
help—she is quite knacky and inland Christa
was adapting well to the coast. Ciaran and I
pushed off and scrambled over the stern board.
We puttered out beyond the little islands and
headed northwest. We looked back at
Creagach, trying to see if its Seal Cave lived up
to its name. We were going very fast so we could
not be sure whether the dark things pointed out

to us by Jill were seals' heads or rocks.

Anthony opened the throttle full and we were fairly bouncing along. We were protected from spray by the windscreen but we were glad of the extra clothes, though the orange jackets made us look like a lot of Disney beetles. Jill's had a little collar and she looked the best, sitting there quietly and enjoying herself a lot. The boat thumped down on the water with a noise like a giant beating a monster carpet. Flocks of black shags rose from the rocks and dived into the water behind us looking for prey. Ciaran pointed out the needle-beaked Arctic tern and choughs with their legs to Christa and told her that there were ravens in the back of Illancrone.

We were passing the east side of the island and the houses were not visible—only the schoolhouse could be seen. Anthony had a pair of binoculars on the shelf beside his wheel. I lifted them and he nodded, making a sign to loop the strap round my neck. He slowed down slightly and I was able to train them on the school. It looked quite derelict—sad looking. Imagine! thinking an empty school sad. What was happening to me? Ciaran took the glasses and had a look. I could see from the way he stiffened slightly that he had seen something, or thought he had. He handed me back the glasses and I returned them to Anthony's shelf. He gave me the thumbs-up sign and increased speed again.

Round the back of Illancrone the sea was rougher and we bounced more. I could see that Christa was a little bit frightened for she sat down beside Jill and began to play with Glinka. The island looked very bleak with neither house nor field. The sea was white round the bottom of the cliffs and seagulls wheeled round and round the shiny black rock. I could well believe that ravens lived there.

Soon, however, we were into the westering sun again and heading for home. We could see the Illancrone street very clearly but there was nothing strange.

"Leave us at the Sound, Anthony," I said. "Mother has given us money to have a drink at the clubhouse."

"Keep off the hard stuff, lads!"

We all laughed except Christa whose face had on its "I don't quite understand" look. Anthony brought the boat neatly alongside the jetty and we all bundled out, glad to feel the warmth of the land again. We jumped and stretched our legs. Anthony called me back.

"Any more word of Multilit?"

"Not since this afternoon."

He laughed and cast off.

There weren't many in the clubhouse when we bought our drinks and sat down in the corner. Christa startled Joe the barman when she ordered a lager.

"Are you sure you're not under-age?"

She gave him a look. "In Germany the whole family is drinking beer."

And that was that!

About eight o'clock we were just deciding to leave when Paddy Carter, Ciaran's father, came in. I like him. He is friendly and doesn't tease and he is very decent about lifts.

"I was sent to fetch you. There is a friend of yours, Ruairi Ó Bláine, left a message at the house. There is a Céilí Mór in the College at Loughanure. Your mam and dad say you can go. So can you, mister. What about you, young Christa? Would you get permission?"

"What, please, is a Céilí Mór?"

"It's a kind of war-dance done by the crazy Irish," said Ciaran.

"But what kind of dancing? Modern or traditional?"

I answered: "Sort of barn-dancing—folk-dancing with special steps and figures."

"There will be young people at it?"

"About our age."

"That is indeed young!"

Suddenly I felt a blaze of anger. She was showing off, trying to seem more sophisticated than we were. She should not have put Joe on the spot, asking for lager like that. I mean, did she really think she was grown up?

"Come on, granny!" I said sharply, wondering why I was so angry and leaving Ciaran to explain.

Christa sat in the front with Mr Carter while Jill sat between Ciaran and me in the back. She lay back with her eyes closed pretending to be asleep. Her arms were round Glinka and she was holding his chain between her teeth. This is a favourite trick of hers—maybe some form of self-hypnosis. I decided to risk it.

"What did you see with the binoculars? The school looked pretty wrecked to me."

Ciaran looked at Jill and whispered, "There was a radio aerial—a new one—fixed to the chimney."

"And what does that mean?"

"I think they are going to guide a boat in, some dark night. They'll store the drugs in some of the houses and they'll bring consignments to Creagach as they need them. Then it's no trouble to get them to Dublin."

"I think I know where they'll bring the stuff

out to Creagach."

"Where?"

"Over on the west, below the bog—a kind of mini Tráigh Dhearg."

"Yeah, I know the place."

Jill had dug a puzzle out of her pocket, one of those moving tile things that after five million moves makes a butterfly or something.

"Mrs Sweeney was talking to Packie when I was playing with Emer. Two men wanted to get his tractor and bogey for two days. But Packie wouldn't let anybody else drive it but himself. Mrs Sweeney was angry because the money was good."

"How much?" asked Ciaran.

"I didn't hear that. I wasn't really listening. Now Glinka, isn't that a pretty butterfly?" She had the damn thing finished!

"Who were the men?"

"I don't know. I told you I wasn't listening. And neither was Glinka. Were you, pet?"

Sometimes I think that both my sisters are nuts. I said that once to Ciaran and he said it was hereditary. I was really impressed. Ciaran isn't exactly a wit. He once showed me a postcard his aunt sent him from Hong Kong. It said too many chinks, not enough armour. He laughed like a hyena but I didn't get it at all.

We had stopped at a kind of crossroads, one path leading to the cottages, the other to the caravans. Christa got out.

"Ciao! Jill; Aufwiedersehen Gary!"

I just nodded.

10
On with the Dance

or the céilí I wore trousers. Apart from when I went to Mass in Kinladen I never wore them in Creagach. They were grey and I put on a green shirt and a silver-grey sweater. Mother suggested a tie, but for a céilí—I mean! I nearly said, "Wise up!"—an expression she hates, and I would have got an ear-wigging. I was glad that Christa was not there; how could I explain that phrase? I could imagine her saying, "Ja, Ohrwurm, I know. Biology is my good subject, but how can you Ohrwurm someone?" Suddenly I felt rotten for losing my temper with her. I would ask her for the first dance and everything would be peachy.

We were going to travel in two cars. The Carters would take the Weisses and Ciaran and I would travel in ours. The Germans wanted to stay for a few sets because it was all "so interessant," but really it was to check that the place was not a dive and that the dance was properly supervised. They need not have worried: the place would be crawling with teachers and there would even be a priest or two. In fact there would be lots of old people at it. Once Christa's parents had had a good look they were all going into Dungloe for drinks. Sometimes I think big people do an awful lot of boozing.

Ciaran and I talked quietly at the back of our car. It was not hard to talk privately: Mother had put on one of her Daniel O'Donnell tapes and was singing as she drove and my father's jaw was clenched so tight that he would not be listening to anything. We both agreed now how the drugs were going to be brought in. A trawler, say, from Scotland would lie off Illancrone on a night when it was really dark and land the stuff on the island. The aerial was for radio contact. When the stuff was safely stored the smugglers could take their time about getting it into Creagach, and then to wherever. Small cargoes could go straight to Kinladen in the catamaran and the white Mercedes could take it to Dublin or Belfast.

"And I'm sure some has already got in like

that." said I.

"Yes, but don't you see; that's all a bit too slow," said Ciaran. "Maybe they haven't stored it on Illancrone at all. Maybe they were just trying the plan out. Could a trawler get into your cove? You know, the other Tráigh Dhearg."

I thought a bit. "With a spring tide they could get her in but they wouldn't have much time. Maybe an hour and a half. Otherwise their boat would be beached till the next tide."

"How are the tides?"

"Well, you saw for yourself today. It was low at six this evening, so full at midnight."

"So it could be any of these nights?"

"Well they are dark enough; the moon's hardly started."

"I think you should tell someone."

"No! a right pair of eejits we'd look."

"What about the Aged Ps?"

"Would you tell yours?"

He shook his head. "Too much trouble; but you said the locals always know what's going on."

"Yes, but if it does not affect them they'll not do much."

"But they're a dangerous crew."

"So we'll keep away from them!"

We had reached the hall and parked beside

the Carters' car. They and the Weisses had gone on in so we followed. We could hear the music and the slithery thump of dancing feet. There is something about céilí music that sounds great at the start; you really want to dance. Even Ciaran started tapping his feet.

The hall was lively with plenty of talent but still room to dance. There was a High-Caul Cap just finishing—one of the harder ones. I never could remember the figures. The Sixteen-Hand Reel was as complicated as I could handle and I needed a really good partner. The girls I knew were all Irish dancers anyway so that was all right. The band was good—two fiddles, an accordeon, a piano and a really class drummer. It was a big night. A lot of the girls were actually wearing dresses and skirts. When the music stopped I looked around for Christa. I saw her mother and waved and she waved back. "Snap!" I thought. The Fear a' Tí announced Corr Aondruma, one I could do. I looked even harder for Christa. Suddenly I saw her standing out in the line, with Roy Blayney! It was a shock. I turned to talk to Ciaran but he was gone too. The music started, the couples advanced and retired, only I was not dancing.

When it was over there was a Haymakers' Jig called. I was determined to ask Christa for this

one but when I got near to where she had been
standing I saw her walk out on the floor with
one of the teachers. She gave me a broad smile
when she saw me. I was blazing. I felt my fists
harden. I just wanted to walk out the door away
from the hall and keep on walking. I sat down,
stuck my hands in my pockets and brooded. I
watched her dancing, of course. I did not take
my eyes off her and, boy, could she dance! You'd
think she had been going to céilís all her life.
And she was so fair and slim and wearing a
white frock that she was outstanding, a Celt
among the Firbolgs! The dance ended with lots
of whoops and cries. Christa walked to the edge
of the crowd to talk again to die Eltern. Ciaran
and Blayney went to join her but huffily, yes I
admit it, huffing like somebody Jill's age, I sat
where I was. The Fear a' Tí announced The
Sweets of May and Rogha na mBan. Now was
her chance. I waited. No move. Then I saw her
talk to Blayney and walk out on the floor. I was
not huffy any more. I was not even angry. I was
suicidal!

I felt a tap on my arm. It was Máire as Blá
Cliath. Of course, I'd like to dance. We weren't
in the same set as Christa but I was aware of her
dancing like St Vitus. Máire was good crack and
I began to enjoy her Irish, just as I love the

Dublin accent when they are speaking English.

It was hot in the hall now and after five dances in a row she was glad to come for mianraí. She was disappointed they hadn't got Ballygowan. "Actually I usually drink Perrier!" I looked at her, rabbit's teeth and all, but I don't think she was showing off.

The O'Donnells, Carters and Weisses were leaving. They came over with Christa and Ciaran to arrange for getting us home at eleven. Blayney came along too. Paddy would come for us at eleven-fifteen since he never went to bed early and knew the roads. Herr Weiss paid for all the drinks and the crisps and "left us to it" as he said in a strong accent. We talked English because of Christa. "Fuair mé cead ó Mhairtín," said Blayney doing the big man. Not that his Irish was all that great but it was better than his German which would make a cat laugh. Ciaran and Máire hit it off straight away and soon there was a good conversation going. A bit fast for Christa, maybe, but she seemed to understand the gist of it. Well it was not Dr Johnson nor Oscar Wilde for Pete's sake! She had heard of Kylie and Jason and knew Bros. She had even heard of Enya. It was, my masters, a right good tourney of wits except for one dud, one fader. Me! I just drank my putrid orange and stayed stumm. No one noticed, of course, except Christa. The MC called the Three Dances and we shuffled our feet a little prior to moving. Christa spoke:

"I make this another 'raya na man.' Gary, will you please dance with me?"

I felt like Kay when the piece of glass fell out of his eye or when Aslan came back to life in Narnia. It was like coming out of an anaesthetic. I followed her on to the floor. The others had explained that this was not a set but a little like the polka or the two-step. We stood facing each other.

"Why are you being so unpleasant?"

I opened my mouth to defend myself but no sound came.

"You have not been nice to me all evening. What have I done?"

I stammered something about losing my temper, being in bad form. She just looked at me with those gentian eyes and then leaned forward to touch my cheek.

"You must know it is you I like best, far more than all the rest!"

I nodded miserably.

"We are again good friends?"

"Oh yes!" I breathed.

She kissed me on the lips so swiftly that no

one seemed to notice. I nearly melted.

It was the best céilí I was ever at. I only had
Christa as partner for one other dance apart
from Na Trí Damhsaí. Then it was like dancing
with a shadow. She moved so well with me that
I could not find her and yet she was there. I took
her and Máire out for the Harvest-Time Jig and
during the swizzes we were both in danger of
taking off. For the rest of the night wherever we
were dancing we had no difficulty in catching
the other's eye. And then it was over and we
were speeding along with Paddy's powerful
headlights lighting up the twisted roads.
Ciaran with rare tact or innocence sat in the
front with his father. Christa and I held hands
and hers was soft and cool. When the car
stopped at the foot of our casán she kissed me
again but so quickly that no one noticed. She
was as darty as a minnow.

11
Across the Bridge

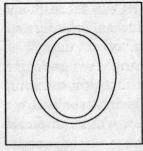

ne of my feet was a centimetre above a tank of piranha, the other was the same distance from a lit candle. Günter was tightening a heavy rope around my neck and the chafed skin was beginning to bleed. The Indian from Glasgow was pulling at my arm, saying, "What this wee mannie needs is an injection." He kept pulling and I was afraid to move. I wondered which would hurt the more, the burning of my sole or the needle sharp teeth of the piranha. Actually it was my arm that was sorest. My mother practically pulled me out of bed.

"Gary O'Donnell! it's nearly ten o'clock. Ciaran's here. He's been up for hours!"

"Right, OK!" I shook the sleep out of my head. "What's he want? Five minutes."

"Now!"

"Bathroom."

I looked in the mirror. There was a definite moustache there. Should I sneak one of my father's disposables? Better not. The sun was shining. Another good day! Yet I could not forget that the holiday would soon be over. And Christa was leaving on Sunday!

Ciaran was reading the cornflakes packet as he ate a second breakfast. He knows what Thiamin, Riboflavin and Niacin actually are.

"Well, my British brother, what's to do today?"

"It's Christa; she's gone!"

"What do you mean 'gone'? Sure we were going to walk across to the Martello Tower and have a picnic." I said this in a normal voice and then quietly so that no one else should hear, "and you were going to get lost for a while!"

"Oh, was I?"

Sometimes he's quite intelligent for a genius.

"Where has she gone?"

"I don't know, mate. While you were snoring in your pit I was looking for starfish down by the old school. The Weiss dormobile came along the road and stopped. They asked me if I had seen Christa. They said she had left a note saying she was going off with that cousin of her mother and she'd be back in the evening.

"Weren't they worried?" I asked, feeling very worried myself.

"Nope! I think they wanted to find Günter to spend the day with them."

"What do you think?"

"I don't know but, I'll tell you something, I don't like it. Oh, by the way, I met someone else."

"Who?"

"Mickey Rodgers. He said he was going to take Oweney Frank's curragh to look at his lobster pots."

"Come on!"

I grabbed a piece of toast and an apple, gulped my tea and shouted to Mother, "We're away!"

"Good!"

"What about lunch?"

"I'm going to Letterkenny with your father and Jill to pick up Mary from the Dublin bus. There's ham and enough potato-salad in the fridge to satisfy even you."

On a thought I dug out from my drawer three bars of chocolate I had being trying not to eat. I stuck them in the pockets of my shorts and ran.

"Let's find Mickey!"

We ran down the path to the tarred road, cut

across Tráigh Dhearg, galloped down by John
the Post's two-storey house and took a short-cut
across the bent to the Sound. We could make out
Mickey in the curragh beyond one of the rocks.
We waved and called until he came in to the slip.

"Mickey," I pointed, "any stir in there?"

"I saw nothing," he said cagily, "but you can
see for yourself from the white water that there
was some craft along here not all that long ago."

"Take us in!"

"Where? to Illancrone?"

I nodded.

"But how will ye get back?"

"You'll come for us this afternoon."

"Arrah, de ye think I've nothing better to do
than to give ye lads pleasure trips?" He paused,
"Why are ye so anxious to get in?"

We told him all we knew and what we
suspected. He shook his head but said nothing.

"I think we should have told the Guards,"
said Ciaran, sounding very correct.

"No, that's not a good idea when ye have
nothing but wild imagination to go on."

"But Mickey, they've got Christa!"

"But you're after tellin' me that Christa went
off wi' that German that has the big dinghy."

"Aye Mickey, but where?"

He scratched his head.

"Look lads, Here's what I'll do. I've a few more pots to lift off Gortladen and I don't mind dropping you on the east strand. If ye haven' managed to get off by three o'clock I'll come in for ye. Do the people know?"

"Mine are gone to Glencolmcille," said Ciaran.

"And mine are in Letterkenny to pick up Mary off the Dublin bus. They'll take their time coming home."

"How is Mary?" asked Mickey and I suddenly realised how he must have felt when she stopped fancying him.

"Grand!" I said as calmly as possible.

We both knelt down in the curragh and with the outboard at full tick we were soon over the edge and wading into the east strand. Mickey pulled away and headed across the bay towards Gortladen. We were on our own.

I had not been much on Illancrone because it is hard to get to and from and hasn't all that much to offer. The street of houses was very spooky and as we walked past them our feet made a clatter. Most of the windows were boarded up, a lot of the thatch had gone to grass and the slates and corrugated iron roofs were in poor condition. It was a real ghost town. Ciaran kept peering in windows and trying doors very gingerly for he was afraid of rats. So was I but I wasn't going to let him know. The day clouded over and we lowered our voices. From this settlement you forgot about the sea and all you could think of was the people, young lads like ourselves who used to live there.

Suddenly Ciaran whispered, "Gary, there's fresh tracks!" He fancies himself sometimes too as Hawkeye, the intrepid Indian Scout. It was then that we heard the noise of a powerful motor. We jumped behind a rock. The catamaran was coming in but from the west and was going to land where we had done on the east strand. I could see McBirney still wearing his baseball cap and another man as tough looking as he. They beached the dinghy and started up the street.

The stranger spoke: "Where's that bloody German?" His accent was English, rough but hard to place.

"Never you mind about pal Günter. He's safe enough and so is the Kraut kid. They're up at the school. Bill's looking after them."

"I don't like involving the girl. It's risky."

"Ah tell ye, there was nae alternative. We need him to deal with Reich and he was fur renegin'. I tellt him a day or two ago we needed her as a kind of insurance policy. I offered tae ventilate his heid fur him if he didnae bring her."

"Well, what's the plan then?"

"Simple: Reich'll bring in his boat to thon wee creek I showed you. I've managed to get a tractor and trailer that Soapy can drive. Two loads will do the whole thing and the fish lorry will be well on the way to Galway before light. And then we'll be in the money!"

Ciaran was hugging himself with delight. It was exactly as we had worked it out. I thought Multilit must be bloody expensive and popular stuff to be worth all this. They moved on. I must admit I was shaking. What the hell to do! We were no match for a gang like this. But we couldn't leave Christa there. If only we had told the Guards. They might not have believed us at the start but we could have kept at them. And I'm sure that we could have persuaded the Weisses that Christa had been kidnapped if we had told them about the scene at Pollnarone. We had to get to the school and try to rescue her. If we could persuade Günter to help us we might hide out by the beach until Mickey came to collect us with the curragh.

"Ciaran, we have to get to that school!"

"They're bound to see us, man! There's not a tree nor a bush we can hide behind. And guys like that aren't stupid; they'll sense we're here."

"We could go by the bridge and get to the school from the back."

"It's too dangerous! Last summer they would hardly let us look at it from below."

"It's the only way!"

The bridge was a thin strip of footway between two high spinks. The sea and the winter storms had worn away all the soil and shale and left a natural arch more than a hundred feet high. The sea was always white below the arch and at sea-level the rocks were very sharp.

We waited five mnutes and then headed west away from the town and beyond the last fields. By this part of the summer Ciaran was fit and we had become very sure-footed and confident. The road petered out and so eventually did the track. We scrambled round by the shore leaping from crag to crag like bloody mountain goats. On the west side there were layered rocks just as in Creagach, something, no doubt, to do with volcanic cooling. Ciaran could have told me but I wasn't in the mood for one of his lectures.

The going was much easier and in about twenty minutes we were under the natural arch only it wasn't a natural arch! The top was gone. Instead of a two foot wide, yard long span there was empty air. It looked just like a railway bridge I saw once being dismantled.

"Well, that's it, Gary; the bog's lost!" (It's very irritating to hear idiomatic Irish phrases in an English accent.)

Things did look bad. It would be seven kinds of madness to try to get across. My groin twitched with frustration.

Ciaran broke the silence: "We'll hide out on the east strand till Mickey comes for us. He'll take us to Kinladen and we can phone the Guards from the Post Office. It's the rational thing to do. We'll do nobody any good by getting ourselves hurt or even killed."

He was right, of course. When you looked up at the broken arch and heard the sound of the waves and the cry of the sea-gulls, the prospect was fearsome. We could stay hidden near the beach till Mickey's curragh came into sight. Then we'd be safe because they wouldn't appear while Mickey was about.

And yet when I thought of Christa in that schoolhouse, maybe tied to a chair, maybe gagged, maybe hurt! I had at least to try.

"Ciaran, I'm going to try. Maybe it's not so wide when you get close to it."

"You're mad, mate! What am I going to tell your mother?"

I gave him a bar and a half of the chocolate. "That's your ration till Mickey comes back."

The he did something that frightened the life out of me. He shook my hand and wished me good luck.

"Reichenbach Falls! eh Holmes?"

He didn't even crack a smile.

It was not hard to scramble up the cliff; the only real danger was from skidding on the screes. There were bits of grass and heather to give a grip and most of the rock was firm. I really like climbing on cliffs but one thing that unnerves me is to see gulls below me, as if to say, "It's too high for me, anyway!"

At last I got to the top and lay on the moss to get my breath and prevent my head getting light. In front was a great view of ocean stretching to Iceland while left was the head of Aranmore and right the coast of Donegal with all the islands and headlands right to Cnoc Fola. I ate the half bar of chocolate and then got up to look at the "bridge" that was now a gap. At first my head and stomach felt strange and I had the feeling that my spine was melting. The wind was strong, making my shirt and shorts flap. The edge of rock where the bridge had been was crumbly. A boulder that had been part of the bridge was stuck not too firmly against the cliff on the other side. The walls of the arch were smooth as if the sea had polished them but how could sea get that high? They say the arch was formed on the the Night of the Big Wind and I reckoned it was one of our recent winter storms that had dislodged the top.

The gap was a bit more than a yard. Jill could have jumped it. I could nearly have stepped it on the ground but up here with the wind and clouds switching the sun on and off it was a different matter. The herring gulls glided way below me, crying like lost cats. I felt the near edge with my foot very tentatively. Not too sound. The far side looked better. I was glad I was wearing walking-shoes and socks and not as usual sandals. What with the excitement of the céilí and the rush out that morning I could not find them. The soles could grip on most things. I had a run up of about four feet to the edge and about a yard of level landing space. What was keeping me? The longer I waited the harder it would be. I stepped as far as I could go, blessed myself and ran forward.

The next second I was on my knees on the far side, my feet over the space and holding on to a bit of rock that I hoped was part of the cliff. As slowly as if I was lying on eggs I pulled myself up and ran across the rest of the arch. I was too

excited and relieved to stop but stumbled,
jumped and slid down to the shore. Then I had
my rest, feeling very pleased with myself and
ate more chocolate.

When I got over the ridge behind the
schoolhouse I lay like a dead man. I could hear
a mumble of voices but could not make out any
words. As I crawled nearer I tried to see
something through the windows but they were
too dirty. I slid down to the out-building they
had used as a toilet. I fancied some of the smell
still clung to the place. Then I saw McBirney
with his giant paw round Ciaran's scrawny
neck push him round to the front and say to
someone I couldn't see in that vile accent of his,
"Would ye look at whut I found? Coming to see
your wee chum, were ye? Well, she'll be verra
glad tae see ye, I hae nae doot!"

12
The Long Swim

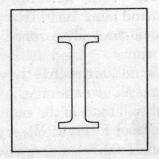 sank to the ground behind the toilet wall. What was I going to do? My mind raced. Actually when I used to read that phrase I never understood it. Now that it was happening I realised what a good description it was. Pictures of Christa, Ciaran, Mickey zipped through my mind but I could not think. I took a deep breath but quietly, had another square of chocolate and thought of nothing but the taste and texture until the last crumb was gone. I was calmer then and able again to think.

There was no point in trying to get into the schoolhouse. I would just end up wi' me wee chums and be no use to anybody. I could do what I told Ciaran to do: lurk about the east strand until Mickey came by with the curragh. But that might be too late. I had to get help. Help was on Creagach or Gortladen. Ergo, as Ciaran would say, I had to get away from Illancrone. I did not really expect that they would have left a handy punt with an outboard lying nicely where no one could see me and I had the feeling that the catamaran would be too well guarded. The alternative was, to swim.

I knew it was a fair bit from Illancrone to the nearest point of the mainland, over a mile, I reckoned. I never swam that length in the sea before. I had done in the pool at home often enough but there was a hell of a difference. The curragh had been pretty lively coming over and I expected that the water would be rough enough. The worst thing was going to be the cold. I ate the rest of the chocolate.

I managed to get down to the beach without being seen. I hid my shirt, shorts and shoes behind a rock and headed into the water in my underpants. It was choppy enough but not all that cold. Well I had been swimming all summer so that did not surprise me. I decided on the old breaststroke. It was not all that fast but it was the one I could keep up longest. After a while I looked back. Illancrone seemed no distance and Creagach looked terribly far away. I decided to head for the beach where we had picked up Mickey. I tried to keep straight but the stream coming round the head of Creagach kept driving me towards the cliffs. I began to panic a little. A few white tops covered my head and shaking the brine free upset my stroke. I waved my arms wildly and felt my stomach tense. "Calm down, O'Donnell! Calm down!" I settled again to steady strokes. Arms out, down and legs up. Arms forward, legs straight and wide. Legs slapped together, move forward. Repeat! And again! And again! A bird flew close by but did not touch me and I did not break my stroke. I looked back again. Illancrone seemed farther away but Creagach did not seem any nearer. Swim! Swim! Still strong enough. Legs going well. Hands and cheeks a little bit cold. The sea was very big and the only noise was the sound of the water and the mewing of the gulls.

All at once I was very bored. I tried to think of Christa but all I could think of was the sea, bubbles passing my ears, splashing in my face. Salt in my mouth. I began to think of poetry, stuff I learned at school:

So all day long the noise of battle roll'd
Among the mountains by the winter sea,
Until King Arthur's table man by man...

Winter sea. It must be cold in winter. Cold. I

was cold now. Not my hands and feet but the small of my back. And my thighs, they were cold. I suddenly felt all wrinkled like a prune. I looked at my hands. They were wrinkled all right! Could I look at my feet? Were they all lines and ridges like my fingers?

Suddenly I was swallowing water. I had lost the stroke again. Tread a bit. Ease the arms. Lean on them like a cushion. Or a pillow. Nice to fall asleep on a pillow. More swallowing of bitter brine. Breaststroke! Arms out! Arms down at exactly 45 degrees. Knees bent ready to spring. Arms out, legs straight. All right again! Really cold now. Was I a blue prune? I laughed but I could not hear any sound. I listened for the sound of an engine but I was alone on the sea. O, a life on the ocean wave, a life on the rolling deep. My neck was too stiff now to turn to see Illancrone but Creagach was nearer. I could see people sitting on the sand, with kids running in and out of the water. I used to run in and out when I was a kid. On days when my father was away, Mother used to bring a flask of coffee and a big bottle of lemonade. She always had two big apples cut in half. One piece for Jill, one for Mary, one for Mammy and one for me. Men always waited. And then she'd open the packet of Custard Creams.

I wasn't cold any more. I was hot, very hot. My feet were burning. They must be raising steam in the water. I liked being warm and cosy. In bed, when I was very young with Mother tucking me in. Night night, sleep tight, don't let the bugs... I was asleep already. Look, Mammy, my eyes are closed... My face felt sore for it was against a tarry rope. I was moving fast now (with my own outboard?) I tried to move my arms but they were too heavy and I was shivering with cold again. I stopped my speeding with a sudden jolt and then I felt the lift of a wave and the smell of wet sand. Somebody was carrying me so I did not open my eyes and then there was a rug. Mother held a glass to my lips and the most horrible burny stuff went down my gullet. It was whiskey or brandy or some of those things. It nearly made me retch but I held it down.

I made an effort and pulled myself together. I shook off the tiredness. I could not understand how I was in bed in the cottage but I was! And everybody was there, Mother, Father, Mickey, Jill and even Mary. Then I remembered. "They've got Ciaran and Christa. They're in the schoolhouse in Illancrone. They're smuggling veterinary drugs. I mean, the gang that have captured them—"

"All right! All right now Gary," said my father in his best professional manner. "Mickey has told us all he knows. He was the one who fished you out of the sea just at the Sound beach. A better catch he never made! The guards will be here soon and they'll, no doubt, want to ask a lot more questions."

"I think they are expecting a boat to come in tonight with the stuff they're smuggling. There will be a good tide tomorrow morning about two o'clock and there is no moon."

"All right," said Father quietly. "Tell us how many of them are there."

"There's at least three. McBirney, a Scotchie, another man who is his boss and somebody called Bill. Oh yes! there's some guy called Soapy who is to drive the tractor. Christa's cousin, or I mean, her mother's cousin, is in the schoolhouse too. I think he's a prisoner as well."

Mickey spoke to my father: "I'll use Oweney's phone again and tell the guards where to meet us. And I have a few more calls to make!"

"Can I come? Please!"

Father looked at Mother and nodded. "Not till you've had some tea and a decent meal," said Mother.

"But I'm not hungry."

"Nevertheless!"

The others left and I dressed in a clean shirt, pullover and my Sunday trousers. When I came down to the kitchen there was freshly-baked soda bread, sausages and chips. I was hungry! The Aged Ps kept looking at me as if I were a bomb about to go off.

"What's the matter? Have I horns?"

Mary smiled quite affectionately for her. "You know, Gary, it was a very brave thing to do. It was very dangerous but very brave." Then she came over and hugged me. The others all joined in. Jill even gave me Glinka to kiss. What could I say? I searched for some smart crack but none came. Besides I seemed to have a lump in my throat.

13
The Great Armada

y the time we got to the Sound, the guards were there with a police launch and they put out immediately. Anthony Doherty brought Mickey, Father and me on the Granuaile. My legs were shaky but I could stand. When we were out a bit I could see we were not alone. Everything that could float seemed to be there—half-deckers from Burtonport and Aranmore, dinghies, punts, curraghs, all waited in a line in the road between Creagach and Gortladen. The police-launch was a little ahead of us and like Mickey the sergeant had his binoculars fixed on Illancrone.

Suddenly the catamaran appeared, dark and evil looking. It seemed to be headed for Kinladen Pier. I suppose it was Mickey who

gave the signal for almost at once the fleet
began moving. They moved line astern until
they were clear of the road. The leader was the
Macha II steered by Mickey's younger brother,
Manus. It headed straight for the catamaran. It
swung east but the line blocked its road and it
whirled west again. We could see the occupants
now clearly: McBirney, the man he called
"Jimmy" (but what did that mean to a
Glaswegian?) and another man I had never
seen before. No Bill, no Günter and no Christa
or Ciaran!

As the catamaran steered west the Macha
turned west after it and drove it east again. The
line followed the flagship so that the enemy
ship now considerably slowed was caught in a
fork. Manus swung the Macha east again and
headed for the last craft in the line, Owney's
curragh with Oweney himself at the tiller. We
were slowed ourselves now following the
Guards because there was not a lot for us to do.
I wanted to make for Illancrone but Anthony
thought it better to wait.

With some further fancy rudderwork Manus
came in behind Oweney. The circle was
complete! Round and round they went in a fine
and narrowing closed curve, while the
catamaran turned and twisted, looking for a

gap. There was none. The boatmen of the Rosses used their old skills and the circle held. I saw McBirney rise with a shotgun and sight it but I was not sure what his target was for the merry-go-round of boats moved faster and tighter. The Garda sergeant raised his loud-hailer to his lips: "Drop that gun and stop your engine. I repeat: drop that weapon and heave to!" McBirney swung round and aimed at the police launch. There was a second of real tension and then he lowered the gun.

The circle parted to let the launch in. The three were taken on board and one of the younger guards took over the catamaran. The Armada began to stand down. There was a great deal of cheering and then they chugged away back to their berths. Now there were just the three craft left in the Sound, the catamaran, the police launch and the Granuaile. We all headed for Illancrone.

After all the excitement the place was dead quiet. I couldn't believe that Bill would not be aware of what was going on. Still the slip was tucked round to the north and facing away from Creagach. We had used the east strand and got the Granuaile with a lot of pulling safely ashore. The launch rode just off shore with the three villains still looking quite intimidating in spite of being handcuffed behind their backs. The guard brought the catamaran in as neat as ninepence. (I heard later he was from the Aran Islands.) Mickey, the young guard, my father and I moved quietly up the street and out along the track to the school. Anthony stayed with his boat. They did not want me to come but I insisted. There was still no sound or sign of movement. Two other guards in plain clothes took their dinghy round to the rocks below the school and were moving quickly up through the old potato-gardens. Mickey thought they were from the Special Branch. They had Uzis but they weren't cocked. Our guard made Mickey, Father and myself lie down behind a ditch close to the school. He motioned the other two round to cover side and rear. Then he kicked open the door and ran in. There was an endless silence and then the sound of a single pistol shot. A tough, scar-faced, red-haired man of about thirty came charging out firing a gun in the air. The uniformed guard appeared at the door and called to the man to stop but he ran on. He must be Bill, I reckoned. He was very close now, a few yards from our ditch. I decided to do one more silly, brave thing—the last I ever intended. I threw myself at his feet. In tripping over me he kicked my ribs. He fell and cracked his head on a rock. The gun had described a nice arc as it flew from his hand and fell on the road in front of him. He didn't move. The guards came carefully down the casán but there was no stir from him. He was out cold.

Garda O'Hare from Inis Oírr (as I learned later) snapped the cuffs on him and we all ran back to the school. The left-hand classroom was full of packets of Multilit but otherwise empty. We opened the other door and there they were! Ciaran and Christa tied and gagged in the big desks and Günter in the teacher's chair. I removed the gag from Christa's face. Her eyes and lips were a little bit swollen but she did not seem to have been hurt. The guards untied everybody and marched Günter down the path to the strand.

Ciaran seemed quite unconcerned. "You see, my dear Watson, exactly as I deduced!" I was too busy watching Christa bending and stretching and doing all those ballet positions that Mary and Jill are always at, to bother to answer. He persisted.

"There is only one thing to be done now."

"And what's that, my dear Holmes?"

"Go to the loo! I've been sat there for hours."

Christa turned her head.

"Wie, bitte?"

I told her. She shouted, "Ich, auch!" and ran after him, laughing. They cheered when we got to the shore and there were all kinds of hugs and kisses when we reached Creagach and met the Weisses.

"You are really quite remarkable children!" said Herr Weiss.

"Pfui! Vati; gar keine Kinder!"

That evening we all piled into cars and drove to Ostán na Rossan in Dungloe. The Garda Superintendent had booked a private room and we had a great feast. Strangely enough I was fit for it. Christa asked the Super, "What about Günter?" He did his cagey policeman act. "Well I don't think we'll be too hard on him. As soon as he found out what they were really smuggling he wanted no part of it."

"It wasn't fertility drugs, was it?" I interjected. (I have always wanted to interject.)

"No," said the Super, "Multilit was really heroin in handy tablet form but they needed him to deal with the East German contact man. They threatened to kill him, of course, and they demanded Christa as a hostage. That explains a lot of the mystery of Illancrone. It might have been simpler if you had told us."

"Would you have believed us, Superintendent?" said Ciaran in his best Brit accent.

"Well now, Ciaran, we might. Sometimes we know more than we are given credit for."

The talk, the questions, the "ohs" and the "ahs" lasted late into the night. Herr Weiss at last rose with a glass of champagne. I noticed that Christa had one too. I looked at Mother but she smiled very sweetly and gave me a bottle of Ballygowan. "Just every bit as fizzy!" she said.

Herr Weiss tapped the table, "I think perhaps a toast to our brave—"

Christa broke in warningly, "Vati!"

"—young people who behaved so well and so courageously, with, I think, a special mention for Gary on account of his mighty leap and marathon swim. Superintendent, do you think there might be a reward?"

"Well now, d'ye know, I never thought. Maybe there might be!"

"So! I now propose a reward for them. We have the use of a large appartment in Salzburg whenever we wish it. Why not, then, let the boys join us in Oesterreich, verzeihung!, Austria, for a week in February, when you have a holiday, nicht wahr? There'll be skiing and skating and all sorts of jolly fun." The Aged Ps and the Carters nodded.

"Wunderbar!" I cried, "but I can't ski!"

"I can teach you!" whispered Christa. So that

was all right.

"Ausgezeichnet!" cried the Weisses and we drank the toast even though we shouldn't have been toasting ourselves.

***

I was up early next day. The Aged Ps were still asleep and even Jill made no move as I passed her door. Illancrone lay bathed in too bright a sun. I could see every house with every slate as clear as with binoculars. It would rain before evening. It did not matter. The party was over. It was closing time. In two days I would be back in school uniform and trying not to boast about the summer adventures. Christa was waiting by the lake.

"We have only a little time," she said, her blue eyes looking at me very seriously. She was wearing a blouse and skirt.

"Sollen wir einen Spaziergang machen?"

"Ja, gut! Dein Deustch wird immer besser!"

We laughed and ran up the steep path to the top of the hill. We looked out at Illancrone.

"It was a great adventure!"

"Ein wunderbares Abenteuer!"

"Will you write to me in Passau?"

"Aber, natürlich! Jede Woche!"

We put our arms round each other and held each other very tight.

"I'll miss you, Irishman."

"Me too."

Her eyes were full of tears. "Schrecklich, der Wind. It makes the eyes water so."

"Till February, my darling!"

She kissed me again.

"Ja," I whispered, "bis nächsten Februar!"

***

It was January. A loathsome mixture of snow and rain lashed the windows of the classroom. Der Kommandant was handing back the German papers.

"O'Donnell," he glinted behind his steel-rims, "this shows a remarkable improvement. Have you been taking lessons?"

"Yes sir!" I answered, with a perfectly straight face. It was easy to keep my face straight since Christa and Ciaran were too far away to giggle.

The Poolbeg Book of Children's Verse

compiled by
Sean McMahon

"Already a classic."
RTE Guide

POOLBEG

Shoes and Ships and Sealing-Wax

A Book of Quotations for Children

compiled by
Sean McMahon

A collection to amuse, surprise and delight.

POOLBEG